This book belongs to:

Published by Charlesbridge
85 Main Street
Watertown, MA 02472
(617) 926-0329
www.charlesbridge.com

Library of Congress Cataloging-in-Publication Data
Alexander, Martha G.
When the new baby comes, I'm moving out / Martha Alexander.
p. cm.
Summary: Oliver is going to be a big brother, and he doesn't like the idea one bit.
SBN-13: 978-1-57091-678-6; ISBN-10: 1-57091-678-0 (reinforced for library use)
bies—Fiction. 2. Parent and child—Fiction. 3. Brothers and sisters—Fiction.] I. Title.
PZ7.A3777   Wh 2006
[E]—dc22
2005009913

Printed in China
(hc) 10 9 8 7 6 5 4 3 2 1

Illustrations recolorized with watercolor and colored pencil
on the pages of a first-edition printing of the original book
Display type and text type set in Roger and New Aster
Color separations by Chroma Graphics, Singapore
Printed and bound by Jade Productions
Production supervision by Brian G. Walker
Designed by Diane M. Earley

MARTHA ALEXANI

When the New Baby
I'm Moving O

All
Ch

[1. B

iꞁꞁi Charlesbridge

For Allen, Scott, Sean, and Isaac, too
—M. A.

"Why are you painting my old high chair?"

"I'm getting it ready for the new baby."

"The new baby! But that's my high chair.
And my crib—you're going to paint that too?

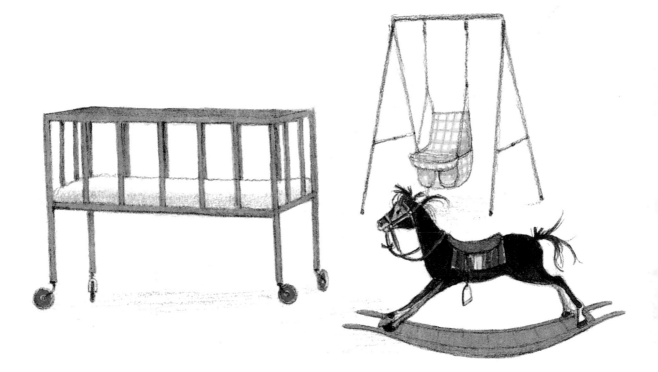

And all my old things!
You didn't even ask me.

I need those things! This was going to be
my spaceship launching pad.

And this is my cage for all my wild animals.
You can't give my cage away.

How would you like it if I gave
your bed away—or your rocking chair?"

"I'm sorry, Oliver. I didn't think
you wanted those old baby things."

"But I do want them—I *do*.
I need them. They're *mine*.

Look! You don't even have a lap anymore.
That baby is taking up all the room,
and it isn't even born yet.

I don't like you anymore.

I'm going to throw you in the garbage can!

And I'll put the lid on too.

And pound it with a stick.

And I won't give you any food.

I'll take you to the dump.
And I'll throw ashes on you.

I'll leave you there.
And you'll be sorry—both of you."

"What a terrible place to leave us—the dump!"

"Well, you could stay here if you want to, and I'll leave.

I'll go live in my tree house.

Or maybe I'll camp in the woods—in my tent."

"I wish you wouldn't go away.
I'd be so very sad and lonely without you."

"You would? You really would miss me?"

"Even more than that.
    I'd be miserable without you.

Who would cut out the cookies
when I roll out the dough? And who
would play hide-and-seek with me?"

"I guess that baby won't be much fun
for you either. I better stay with you."

"You know, Oliver, big brothers get to do lots of very special things."

"They do?"

"You bet they do!"

"Hurry up, baby, I have lots of plans.
I can't wait to be a big brother."